The Running, Jumping, Throwing, Sliding, Racing, Climbing Book

Original English language edition published under the title of
ANIMAL GRANDSTAND
by The Hamlyn Publishing Group Limited
© Copyright Piero Dami Editore 1973 & Presse Bureau Junior
© Copyright The Hamlyn Publishing Group Limited 1974
First published in the United States by Grosset & Dunlap, Inc. 1975
Text, U.S. edition Copyright © 1975 by Grosset & Dunlap, Inc.
All Rights Reserved.
Library of Congress Catalog Card Number: 74-17717
ISBN: 0-448-11912-9 (Trade Edition)
ISBN: 0-448-13246-X (Library Edition)
Printed in the United States of America.

The Running, Jumping, Throwing, Sliding, Racing, Climbing Book

Pictures by Anthony Lupatelli

Verses by Oscar Weigle

GROSSET & DUNLAP
PUBLISHERS • NEW YORK

Soccer

Onto the soccer field they go—
All of these players in a row.

A mighty kick sends the ball through the net.
It moves through the air like a fast-flying jet.

This time the ball strikes the net, and then
Bounces right back to the player again.

The ball goes into the net—and it's fair—
But can you believe how it ever got there?

If you can't kick the ball, then blow it along,
But first be quite certain your breath is strong!

Hooray for our team
And our superstar!
Loud applause and cheers
Come from near and far.

Boxing

This boxer has burst his punching bag,
And he thought he was only playing "Tag!"

A left to the body,
A right to the chin.
That's exactly the way
A boxer can win.

Ladies and gentlemen,
This is the night
Of the Battling Bruisers'
Heavyweight Fight.

A powerful blow
Puts one on the ropes,
But a corner post
Ends the other's hopes.

Tennis

A tennis match played
Between Mouse and Giraffe?
Now, that's surely enough
To make anyone laugh!

When this penguin tried hard
To serve an egg o'er the net,
He wound up, instead,
With an omelette!

This ostrich must be a nervous wreck.
Swallowing a ball—what a pain in the neck!

A mouthful of tennis balls—
That comes in handy.
Do you suppose Mr. Pelican
Would rather have candy?

Mr. Octopus can handle
Five racquets or more,
But after the game is over,
His arms are awfully sore!

Cycling

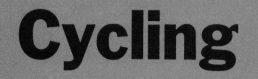

Freddy Fox thinks
It's a terrible bore
Delivering goods
From the grocery store.

What he'd like to do
Is set the pace
In a super-exciting
Bicycle race.

Freddy starts training
With Porky Pig,
A champion cyclist
Who always "wins big."

But then Porky also
Enters the race,
And wins, of course.
Freddy Fox "loses face."

Swimming

This elephant wants to learn how to swim
But he just can't learn unless someone helps him.

The backstroke is easy,
Or so it would seem,
When a self-contained "blower"
Provides a jet stream.

One day a toy boat
That is drifting free
Moves far from the shore,
Drifting out toward the sea.

The elephant swims toward it.
Amazing! He's not sinking!
Perhaps he found it wasn't hard,
Or he did it without thinking.

For his good deed the elephant
Deserves a loving cup.
But he didn't even have to swim.
(He's able to stand up!)

Basketball

It is said that the game
Of basketball
Is best played by players
Who are very tall.

Here's a player
Who is very large,
And the way to win,
He says, is to charge!

A mouse often looks
For something to nibble.
In this case, you see,
He's found something to dribble.

Take a shot at the hoop,
Try to toss the ball in.
Do it often enough
And your team's sure to win.

Skiing

Put ‘on your skis
And head for the slopes.
It helps if there’s snow,
’Cause you can’t ski on hopes.

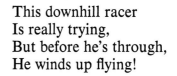

This downhill racer
Is really trying,
But before he's through,
He winds up flying!

Well, that was just one
Of those funny things.
"Now, here's an airplane—
You've earned your wings."

Auto Racing

If you want to run racing cars
At daredevil speed,
A tankful of gasoline
Is what you will need.

When you're speeding along
Like a house afire,
It helps not at all
To have a blown-out tire.

The race is lost
And the rain pours down.
It's enough to make
Almost anyone frown.

It's an obstacle course,
Of that we are sure.
There are rivers to cross,
And—there's a detour.

Don't take a wrong turn.
If you do, take a look
At one luckless driver
Who wound up on a hook!

Sailing

The sailing ships are set to race,
So give them lots of room.
The signal is given for the start—
A shot from the cannon: BOOM!

Over the water
The boats skim today,
And over and over,
In more than one way!

What a sad predicament
For such a teeny mouse!
It might have been much better
If he'd never left his house.

All's well that ends well.
Yes, everything is fine,
As Mousie passes Elephant
Across the finish line.

Mountain Climbing

Why does one climb a mountain
In weather foul or fair?
The answer's always given:
"Just because it's there."

To rescue mountain climbers
Is Ranger Bear's brave game,
But when one must climb high ladders,
Well, that's simply not the same.

Football

What makes a football superstar?
And what must he do to shine?
He must pass, run with, or kick the ball
To the other team's goal line.

When it rains, the field is muddy.
The ground looks like a ditch.
And so, when the game is over,
Who can tell which team is which?

Wrestling

Officer Elephant seems to be slow,
So the Police Chief says to him,
"The way to shape up is for you to go
To the ABC Wrestling Gym."

Now, Elephant doesn't know his own strength,
And a hold with his trunk is "no fair."
The instructor thinks he should leave the gym,
And stay far away from there.

There are three mean robbers stealing,
Taking lots of loot to a van.
Elephant shouts, "You're under arrest!"
Then he "holds" them, as only he can.

For his good work capturing robbers
He is given a medal of gold,
But perhaps it is also presented
For the super-elephant hold!

Gliding

If you would like to soar like a bird,
Get into a glider and go . . .
But because a glider has no engine at all,
Of course, you'll first need a tow.

Riding on currents of air in the sky,
The glider moves down when they're cold.
And when they are warm, the glider soars up;
At least, that's what pilots are told.

There isn't much fun in waiting
For the dinner guest to show up,
So since he's still "up in the air,"
We'll SEND him his loving cup!

Diving

Plain or fancy diving
Into a swimming pool
Is a healthful exercise
And helps to keep you cool.

When this hulky elephant
(Who is not so very skilled)
Hurls himself into the pool,
It then must be refilled!

As Mr. Elephant starts his dive,
The judges are now all set.
A see-through wall has been built there
So that no one will get wet.

Bobsledding

Mr. Hippo's on a bobsled team,
And it seems like lots of fun,
But along the way he's off the sled,
Stuck in the middle of the run!

The other sled comes down the run,
And soon it picks up speed,
Because Mr. Hippo has been picked up, too,
A winning advantage, indeed!

Weight Lifting

Lots of strength is needed
To lift things into a van.
You are, indeed, a weightlifter
When you are a moving man.

So if you lift more weights, like this,
And do that without fuss,
You may discover one fine day
You can lift a loaded bus!

Baseball

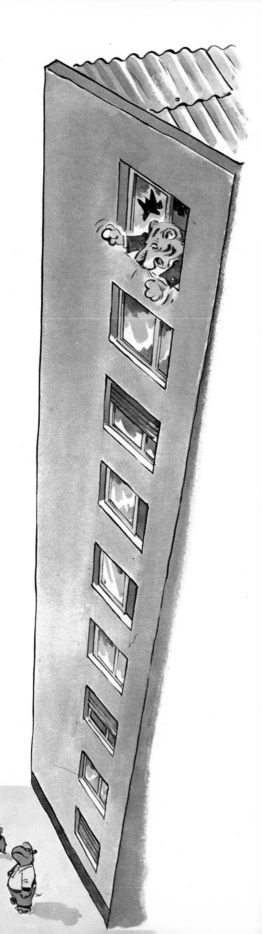

On the big baseball diamond
"Play ball!" is the cry.
The bat strikes the ball hard,
And the ball flies quite high.

Before the ball returns to earth,
The batter will buy some ice cream,
Then run around the bases once.
Hooray! Home run for the team!

Track Cycling

Round and round the cyclists go,
Round and round the track.
The elephant leads by a trunk,
Mr. Mouse is at his back.

Mr. Mouse now pedals hard
And in a sprint of speed
He overtakes the others.
Now HE is in the lead.

Sometimes these lazy cyclists
Would rather not race, but creep,
So when at last they finish the race,
The judges are all asleep!

Figure Skating

When Kitty spilled a can of paint
While skating on the ice,
Her tail became a paintbrush.
Thought she: "That's very nice!"

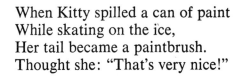

When other skaters did their leaps
And pirouettes so fine,
Kitty scored the highest points
For her unusual design!

Running

On the mark these racers wait
For the starting gun.
BANG! It's fired. Now they're off.
Hooray! The leopard won!

The rhino doesn't know when to stop,
And, of course, he's very large;
So if he doesn't win every race,
He usually wins every charge!

Golf

A hole in the ground is the target—
Golfers hit a white ball and then
They move along to the next hole
And hit that golf ball again.

The ball sometimes lands in a sand trap,
But the golfer will always pursue.
Should it even land on a lily pad,
He may get to it by a canoe.

After the game is over,
It's time for something cool.
Ah, there's nothing so relaxing
As a dip in the swimming pool!

Speedboat Racing

Some people like to tinker
With nuts and bolts and such;
And if you're speedboat racing,
It matters very much.

This cabin cruiser is a dream—
The finest one afloat,
But when it's overloaded,
It's not a racing boat!

A fan is tied to the roof of the boat
To make it jet-propelled.
Isn't this the silliest race
Anyone has ever beheld?

Ice Hockey

Hockey is a game of skill
That's played upon the ice,
But now and then the game gets rough,
And that's not really nice.

Who wants to play with ruffians
Whose specialty is fights?
This team has the answer—
Come dressed as armored knights!

MUSEUM

Motorcycling

Racing motorcyclists
Stir up quite a breeze,
And sometimes (take notice)
They have injuries.

Sometimes, though, they are in luck—
At least, here, so it seems.
Instead of knocks and bruises,
They wind up with ice creams!

Walking

A walking race, you may be sure,
Is not for everyone,
But if you like the exercise,
You might say it's great fun.

There are some who'd rather eat than walk,
And Mouse is one of these.
If you should ask what he likes best,
He'd squeak, "A piece of cheese!"

When Giraffe sees the moving basket
Carrying Mouse along through the air,
He is right to say to the judges,
"Now, that simply is not fair!"

Throwing

The hammer-throw and the javelin-throw
Are done by some athletes.
You must see them to believe them—
These most outstanding feats.

A strong arm comes in handy
For throwing anything,
So first be sure to exercise,
And then—well, have a fling!

Jumping

Do these creatures think they are
Acrobats or circus clowns?
They're training to be "jumping jacks,"
So they have their ups and downs.

If you're not a hopping bunny
Or a leaping kangaroo,
Why not try pole-vaulting?
It's the next-best thing to do.

Gymnastics

Some athletes are quite graceful
As they "work out" at a gym,
But that's not true of Hippo—
Exercise is not for him.

Still, there's a place for Hippo
Where he can go quite far.
His weight upon a springboard
Makes him a circus star.